MW01126055

Reivenge

Queen Novels

Copyright © 2019 Brown Publishing Co

All rights reserved.

ISBN:9781096907190

DEDICATION

This book is dedicated to all of A Hot Summer's fans who supported the first book and inspired the sequel. A special dedication to S. Lord, D. Teague Jr., & EA Brown for being the motivation to break through ceilings.

Table of Contents

ACKNOWLEDGMENTS

Thank you to everyone who not only bought, but read the first series, A Hot Summer. A special thank you to S.Guidry who pushed sales even when this book was just a hobby.
The readers are the one who made this book possible, who pushed me to see myself as an author.

1 The Beginning

On the drive back to the house I started thinking about what Reina had used to poison me, but then it hit me. I had missed my period.

It all started to make sense, the nausea, fainting, vomiting. It could not have come at a better time, I just needed to make sure.

I pulled off on the next exit and headed toward the neighborhood Walmart. I searched hurriedly through the isles in search of a pregnancy test. I finally found it located near the sanitary napkins.

I rushed to the line and paid for it. It was no way that I was going to wait until I was back at the house to find out. I asked an associate where the restroom was located and headed toward it.

When I got in the restroom, I read the directions on the box, pulled down my pants and pissed on the stick, concentrating so I wouldn't get any pee on the window part.

I sat the test on the napkin disposal in the stall and I waited. It wasn't even two minutes before the line appeared to indicate the test was done correctly.

A minute later another line to form a plus.

Fuck, I'm pregnant with TJ's baby!

I slipped the test in my purse, headed out the stall to wash my hands and out of the bathroom toward the door to exit the store.

I was numb. There were no feelings of fear, happiness, sadness, nothing. It was a numbness that I had never felt.

When I got in the car, I called TJ.

"Hello?" the piece of shit answered.

"Hey, I need to see you" I told him "where are you?"

"I'm at the clinic handling business" he replied.

"I'll meet you at the East Parlor, twenty minutes" I said before I hung up. I headed toward the East Parlor forming my plan in my head. That would be the last time anyone would ever play me like a fool. I was going to show everybody just who they were fucking with and what I was capable of and they could thank Reina for that.

I was about to introduce them to a monster.

When I arrived at the East Parlor, I was greeted by the one of the distros. "Park the car" I said as I handed him the keys and walked into the clinic. He was clearly surprised at my lack of greeting which he wasn't used to.

I escorted myself through the parlor and to my private suite. Once in, I picked up the phone and advised that I wanted a double desert when my guest arrived. Then I undressed to show just my hot pink lace panties and bra. I let my hair down and waited for TJ to arrive.

After about ten minutes, he walked in and was clearly pleasantly surprised when he saw me.

Before he could close the door to the suite, I walked over to him half naked and licked his lips, then I licked his ear and after that his neck. While I was licking his ear, I ran the palm of my hand down the front of his pants where I could feel his dick finding an erect position and I moaned a little to let him know that I felt it.

It drove him crazy when I moaned. He picked me up to carry me toward the couch and I saw the deserts being served. Both girls were gorgeous, but one stood out.

She was light skinned with green eyes and multiple tattoos that formed a mule on her body. She was particularly petite and had long straight hair. She had her hair pinned up in a high ponytail that displayed the beginning of her extensive butterfly vine work that covered her entire body.

Her bronzed skin made the colors on the work vivid as if she were a portrait.

She had plump titties that sat up by themselves with a flat belly and a small round botty.

Her pussy had no hair, like it had been waxed and I was instantly turned on the moment I laid eyes on her. I wanted her.

When TJ sat me on the couch, I motioned for her to come to me. When she walked over, I leaned over and kissed her on her soft lips. She was very timid which was even more appealing.

"Have you ever been with a woman?" I asked her intrigued by her shock and timid look from my kiss.

TJ moved my panties to the side and started fingering me softly while I spoke to her.

"No Madam, but I'm here to serve you" she answered in a sweet innocent voice.

I moved TJ's hand and I got down from the top of the couch. I took her hand and helped her on to the couch to take my place where I was sitting.

"What makes you feel good?" I asked her.

"I'm here to serve you Madam" she responded, and I smiled at her.

"Suck on her titties" I told TJ as I continued to smile at her.

TJ started to softly suck on one of her titties and she began to loosen up.

I spread her legs open kneeled down in front of her and licked her pussy. She gave such an intense moan that my pussy wet up and I licked her again, searching for her clit. I licked her pussy like I missed it while TJ sucked her titties passionately.

She pushed down on my tongue and it drove me wild. I inserted my index and middle finger into her pussy while I licked her clit softly and passionately and she pushed up and down again my fingers and my tongue. She groaned in pleasure and leaned her head back while lifting her bottom searching for more.

Her breathing intensified and the volume of her moans became louder. She tried to push away but I fingered her harder and sucked her clit. She lost herself in her pleasure and my mouth filled with the sweet juices of her pleasure.

I pulled my fingers out of her and I tongue kissed TJ to share the sweetness of her cum while I unbuttoned his shirt and pants, pulling them off so hard that I ripped several buttons.

He positioned me next to the girl and I pushed her shoulder to slide her down the couch to the floor so that she was positioned with her face on front of TJ's dick.

Then I stood up for him and he pulled my panties off and begin to passionately lick my pussy while she sucked on his dick.

He moaned from the pleasure she was giving him, and I moaned from the feeling of his soft tongue. He inserted his index and middle finger into my ass as he was eating my pussy and I groaned of excitement.

I motioned the other dessert over to and pulled her on to the couch to suck on my titties. She sucked them perfectly and I grabbed her head as TJ provided immense pleasure to my pussy with his tongue.

I found myself caught up in the pleasure of the warmth of his tongue to my clit and I began to rock into his mouth while beginning to pull the hair of the dessert from all the excitement I was feeling.

TJ let out a groan of pleasure because the rock caused his dick to immense into the throat of his pleasure and she let out a slight choking sound. Just then I felt an overwhelming urge to hold on to a heightened sensation that overtook my body and I grabbed his head pushing it into my pussy fiercely and holding it so that he could not move at all.

I climaxed to the highest point and filled his mouth with the sensual juices that he so eagerly searched for. I could tell from his jolt of surprise that my body had given more cum in his mouth than he'd ever experienced. He was overwhelmed by the juices that filled his mouth and leaked intensely from his face.

He pulled his dick from the mouth of the first desert and flipped me over on the couch and stuck his dick in me aggressively. The look on his face was more than adequate to show that he was pleased with the extreme wetness that my pussy provided him.

He fucked me while the deserts kneeled on the side of the couch watching, waiting for a directive to move. But I let him have me to himself.

He moaned in intense pleasure, licking my nipples, and kissing my neck as he repeated the moving of his dick in and out of my pussy and I watched him.

He enjoyed it so much that he was lost in pleasure and didn't notice me watching him without cease.

The pleasure overcame him, and he started speaking a language of an intense pleasure that reminded me of Pig Latin before he let his cum fill me up inside.

As his dick softened, he fell on me in exhaustion and I nodded for the desserts to prepare the cleaning utensils.
They both exited the room for a few moments, before returning with the cleaning supplies.

I moved TJ off me and allowed them to clean my pussy of the mess. While they were cleaning, two other entrees joined the room and began to sanitize the areas around where we had enjoyed each other.

When they were done with me, they cleaned TJ while he lye on his back with his eyes closed. I dressed myself while he was being cleaned while watching him intently.

After his cleaning was complete, he opened his eyes and looked at me with a smile. I smiled back at him, but definitely not for the reason he was smiling.

He was happy, satisfied. I was about to snatch that shit right out of his hand.

"What?" he asked, curious about why I was smiling?

"What, what?" I asked him, acting like I didn't know why he was asking me such a weird question.

"Summer, you're smiling. It's been a long time since I've seen you smile like that" he said.

I just shrugged and walked over to him where I took a seat. I grabbed his hand and he lifted mine to kiss it.

"Can I ask you a question?" I asked him.

"You can ask me anything" he replied.

"Will you help me kill Reina?" I asked him sternly.

"Whatever you need me to do, I'm here for you" he said.

"Well, that's good. I was worried that you'd be hesitant to kill your sister" I replied casually.

TJ was silent, it was the first time that I'd ever seen him nervous. He fidgeted uncomfortably and scrambled around in his brain for something to say.

"I mean, I'm sure you would benefit from it just as much as I would, considering the fact that you both are planning to kill me."

Silence.

TJ looked like he had seen a ghost. I could tell that he was debating on whether to strangle me or make a run for the exit.

"I see you're at a loss for words, so I'll just help make this decision for you. We're going to have a baby. I don't think Reina will like that very much, especially considering that your job was to keep me under control."

Nothing.

He was still quiet. He didn't blink. He adjusted and readjusted his body on the couch as if something were sticking him.

"I found out that I was pregnant after I went to see my sister, Maddy.

At first I thought Sydney had poisoned me, but then I realized, I hadn't gotten a period so I went to the store and grabbed a test" I told him as if we were engaging in a normal conversation.

"The cat was out of the bag when I heard Sydney's last name Tyson. Did you not think I'd put 2 and 2 together? I know you both think you had me fooled and that was a part of my plan."

"But this baby changes things for me, for us. We're going to take over your sister's business, after we kill her" I finished.

TJ cleared his throat, but even as his words came out the nervousness could still be heard. "Summer, Syd made me go along with it. I didn't want to hurt you, or even be involved" he started.

"TJ save your bullshit. I don't want to hear it and I'm sick of the lies" I said firmly. "You were a willing participant and I'm not concerned with it. If you won't help me kill Sydney, then I'll kill your baby.

Choose" I told him matter of factly.

"I'll do it. Please, don't hurt my baby Summer. That's a part of me growing inside of you. It's the only blood family I have if what you're saying is true." I got up, walked over to my purse and pulled the pregnancy test from it. I handed it to him.

"What I'm saying is very true" I told him while handing it to him.

"When?" he asked me with total submission. "She needs to die soon" I told him. "Once she finds out I'm pregnant, she will want to kill me."

"Ok, how do you want to do it?" he asked.

I laid out the plan for him, explaining to him that I was going to tell Reina that I was pregnant and the scenarios that would likely happen. I didn't plan to tell Reina the baby was TJ's but to leave the assumption that it could have been Ro's baby. I had never told her that TJ was the only one I'd ever fucked without a condom and I knew that she would assume that it was Ro's baby.

The anger would overwhelm her strategy and that is what I depended on. It was the only way to win. Reina was far too smart and if she was thinking clearly there would be no way to fool her, even with TJ's help.

When I was done with TJ, I was going to kill him and bury him next to his sister, and then his baby. For the first time I was in the winner's chair for real.

We headed out the parlor, TJ following behind me like a wet puppy, grasping at my every command. In this position he reminded me of Ro and a part of me wanted to feel sorry for him, but I knew I couldn't.

This was the same man that planned to kill me. He had spent so much time plotting with that crazy bitch Reina and had ended up being in the worst position.

When we got to my car, he opened the door for me. I seated myself in the car and looked out at him.

"Summer, I just want to say that I'm sorry, for everything" TJ said to me.

I grabbed the door handle from on the side of him and closed the car door in his face.

I started up the car and pulled off.

He was sorry?! Who really gives a fuck? I know he didn't think I did. It was evident that he realized that he'd lost control and was desperate to do whatever he could to get it back.

I headed to the house. As I was driving, I dialed Reina's number.

"Hello?" she asked in an unusual tone of uncertainty.

The only assumption was that TJ had already spoken to her. I was certain that he had told her about the baby, but I wasn't sure if he had told her my plan.

It was only one way to find out.

"Hi Rei, are you home? I have some exciting news to share with you!" I said in the most exciting voice that I could muster up.

"Yea, I'm here. I'll see you soon" she said as she hung up the phone.

She knows and she's not happy.

It gave me even greater pleasure to know. I was going to need some help so I put in a call to an old friend.

"Trice, hi, it's Summer."

I told Trice everything and gave her the portion of the plan that I needed her for. I needed Trice because Reina wanted her badly. Many times, when

I would have Trice I'd come back and tell her about it. I'd describe the fucking in detail and Reina would be excited.

She told me she wanted Trice, but I wouldn't let her have her. Trice was something that I kept for myself and Reina knew that Trice would not pleasure her unless I told her to. Trice was in love with me.
Reina's desire for Trice was going to give me the advantage. Trice was damn near irresistible.

When I finally pulled up to the house, I saw that Trice was already awaiting my arrival. When she saw me step out of the car, she walked over to meet me.
She was dressed in an all-black Moschino jumper that was sheer at the top. The jumper had a made-on waist belt that was black with white lettering that read Moschino all the way around.
She didn't have on a bra and had nothing covering her nipples. The jumper provided a full view of her perfect perky titties.
Her jumper was accompanied by some white open toe Jimmy Choo's that complimented her long legs.
Her hair was pulled back in a long fish tail braid with light strands falling.

She wore a smoky eye with a red lip, and she looked beautiful. Her dark skin glistened from the moisturizer that she used, and she smelled of Chanel No 5 perfume.

Trice had exceeded my expectations and I knew that it would be easy for her with Reina. As a matter of fact, I counted on it.

She made my pussy wet the moment I laid eyes on her so I knew that she would do the same for Reina.
I grabbed Trice's hand and walked beside her on the way to the door of the house.

When I opened the front door, I could see that Reina was waiting in the library drinking tea as she normally did.

"Reina?" I called out for her.

She came out the library and the minute she saw Trice she lit up like a firecracker.

"Rei, you know Trice! I thought I'd bring her as part of the celebration for the news I want to share" I told her.

Reina didn't take her eyes off Trice as I was talking. *She's right where I need her to be!*

"Rei! I'm going to have a baby!" I screamed in excitement.

Reina turned from Trice to me and her facial expression told me that she had no idea. TJ hadn't spoken to her.

She was totally stunned by the news.

"And, as a celebration, I thought I'd give you a treat" I continued as if I didn't even notice her shocked expression.

Trice walked over and took her hand leading her toward the stairwell. Reina didn't say anything. She followed Trice in silence.

"Enjoy Trice and enjoy your treat Aunt Rei!" I said.

It must have thrown her off because she stopped and turned to look at me.

"What do you mean? Why are you calling me that?" she asked nervously.

"Rei, we've been friends for years, you're more like my sister and going to raise this baby to call you Auntie" I said.

"By who?" Reina asked.

"It's a long story. I think I've been pregnant for a while and didn't know it. I wasn't expecting it, but it's definitely a blessing! This baby will be the legacy that lives on!" I told her.

"Go, enjoy your gift, we'll talk later!" I said giving her the biggest smile ever.

For the first time I saw Reina vulnerable. She was confused, maybe upset, and nervous. It was clear that she had just received confirmation that her plan was fucked up.

Trice tugged Reina's arm to continue leading her upstairs and Reina complied.

I watched as they walked upstairs imagining what kind of pleasure Trice was about to give Reina.

Once they had disappeared from the stairwell, I headed upstairs toward my room to call TJ and get the plan in motion.

When I reached the end of the hall that had the exit to my bedroom's wing, I heard a loud noise comparable to a powerful firecracker, and I spun around to see what it was.

That's when I saw her drop to the floor slowly, blood running out of her mouth, and a tear from her eye as she grasped for air and reached out to me.

I ran over to her in panic and my heart dropped to the floor. I picked up the phone and hit send to call the last number I had called.

I heard TJ answer.

"Hello?" "Summer?"

I screamed in terror, "She killed her, she killed Trice!", and I could hear TJ screaming my name.

"Summer, I'm on my way!" he screamed.

But I knew that he would be too late. When he arrived, I'd be there, probably dead with his baby lying next to Trice.

"Summer, why don't you go ahead and hang the phone up" Reina said in a voice that I had never heard before.

I pressed end on the call and looked up and suddenly I was looking into the barrel of a black 9MM, Reina at the other end of it.

"You see Summer, you know what your fucking problem is? You think you're smarter than you really are. That's the disappointing fact about life. When you think you've got it all figured out, POW, nothing is ever what you thought it would be." Reina said while pointing the 9MM directly toward my head.

Oh shit, I'm going to die, I thought to myself. How had I been so naïve to think that I could beat Reina? She had been at this a lot longer than me. She was queen of a goddamn drug and sex empire. This bitch had killed her own father for crying out loud! I knew that she wouldn't hesitate to blow my fucking brains right across the floor.

"Reina, please, don't. I'm pregnant. Tell me how to make this right and I swear I will!" I pleaded looking into her ice-cold eyes. I was looking for any sign of affection for me and if any remained, I couldn't find it.

"Summer, you had your chance. I tried to love you and make you a better person than my mother. But, you're all the same" she said waiving the 9mm carelessly in my face.

"Was it too much to ask you to love me? I've given you everything! All I wanted was you to love me and treat me like family" Reina shouted. "But no, Maddie has corrupted you, and you're a plague to this earth, just like her." "She abandoned me, for you, because she loved you most, and now, I'm going to take what she loves most" Reina laughed in a tone that made my soul shiver.

I was scared. Reina was going to kill me just like she killed Trice and leave me to lie with her. She'd probably just have one of the Governors dispose of my body, maybe next to Ro's body. I started to cry and scream for mercy.

Reina let off a bullet from the 9mm that was so loud that it probably perforated my eardrum. I didn't know if she had shot me. I was scared to look. When I looked up, I saw that she had put another bullet into Trice who was gasping for air.

I screamed again "Stop, please Reina!"
"Shut the fuck up Summer. If you make another fucking sound, I will shoot you in one limb until I run out of limbs to shoot you in." "Besides, not to worry, you're going to stick around for a little bit. I will have the pleasure of watching Maddie crumble as she watches the only person, she's ever loved

taken from her." "This is all of your fault! I wanted to do this another way Summer, but you just wouldn't cooperate" Reina said with a ghostly teary eye.

Reina pulled me up by my hair and began to drag me down the hall toward the library. She pressed the metal tip of the 9mm forcefully on my temple and I walked with no resistance.

Her grip on my hair was so tight that I would not have been the least bit surprised if it would have detached from my head the moment, she let it go. I sobbed silently as I was instructed not to make a sound.

When we go to the library, she let my hair go and motioned for me to sit down on the couch. I had been in this very library with her many times and it had never seemed so cold and creepy. I felt like it was a dungeon and I was more scared than I had ever been. I prayed for TJ to get there, to save me. He was my only option at that point. Even if she killed him, perhaps I would have the chance to escape. At that very moment I felt nauseous and I leaned over the side of the couch a vomited.

Reina sat across from me on the other couch and watched me, totally unbothered by the fact that I was puking my brains out. She didn't move or say a word. When I came up for air, I met her cold stare. It startled me so much that I looked away quickly and found a spot on the bookshelf to occupy myself.

Then I heard it, the front door. Someone had come through the front door! She looked at me as if she dared me to scream. Reina got up and left the library.

What was she waiting on to kill me? Was she going to torture me first? I looked around the room frantically for a plan to escape, or something I could use to defend myself long enough to get away. I was afraid to move, and I felt paralyzed. I knew it was the fear that wouldn't allow me to get up from the couch and find a way to fight.

"You're going to die here, unless you get up and go now!" I said in a whisper to myself. I got up from the couch and tiptoed to the door of the library. I could hear voices, but the conversation was in whisper.

I quickly turned around and ran toward the drawers in the library. I knew that Reina kept a pistol in there somewhere. That was the only chance I had, find the pistol, kill this crazy bitch, and get out of there. It had to happen quick.

I couldn't find anything in the drawers that were unlocked. It had to be in the bottom drawer. It was locked and I had no idea where the key was. But then, I saw it, sitting right next to a plant on the desk. It was one of the burner cell phones. I picked the phone up and dialed.

"The Gates residence" the voice answered on the other end. "Hi, I need to speak with Madelyn Gates, it's an emergency please" I said to the voice on the other end. "One moment, I'll get her for you."

A few moments later I heard her voice, "Hello?" "Maddie, it's me. I need help" I whispered through my tears of relief that she was home. "Summer, what's the matter?"
"Reina is going to kill me. I'm at her house. She killed someone already and she's going to kill me. Please help me. I'm going to die. I'm scared!" I blurted out in a whisper.

"Summer, I'm coming. Stall her, fight back, do what you can! Leave this phone on and I'll trace your location" Maddie said.

I heard footsteps coming down the corridor toward the library so I sat the phone down but clicked the side button so the light would go off and ran to the couch to sit down. I began to cry. I wasn't sure if I'd be able to hold off until Maddie got there. I didn't know if I was going to die.

Reina walked through the door of the library fast and fierce toward me. "Summer, you just can't seem to mind your fucking manners" she said as she lifted her hand that was holding the 9mm and swung it to meet my head with a mean crash that left me unconscious

"Summer..Summer, are you alright?" I could hear the voice, but my head hurt so bad that I cried out in pain. I tried to open my eyes and focus them. I didn't know where I was or what happened. My head was screeching in pain and I felt the gentle hand pick up my head and place it on a soft pillow.

I opened my eyes to see and as I looked around, I realized that I did not recognize where I was. But I saw a familiar face and it brought some comfort that maybe I had dreamt it all. "TJ?" I asked in a whisper, as it was all that my breath would let go besides the groan of pain.

"Baby, be careful, don't try to speak" he said as he looked at me with a sadness in his eyes. "Are you feeling alright?" he asked in a concerning voice.

"Yes, I've never been better" I whispered sarcastically. "Where am I?"
"Reina has us locked in a room behind one of the walls in her house" he said.

Just then I jolted my eyes completely open in fear and looked around. I wasn't familiar with the place that I was in and fairly alarmed that there was a door with only one way out and no window.

"Omg, TJ, what are we going to do? She's going to kill us" I cried hysterically.
"Summer, calm down. I'll figure something out" he said, getting up from the bedside and pacing the small room.

Looking at TJ so vulnerable made me realize that he wouldn't be able to save us, and nobody would be able to find us. I had no idea that Reina even had rooms behind the wall of a house that I had lived in for years. I closed my eyes and wept.

"Summer, tell me everything. Did she say anything that could give us a clue to get us out of here?"

"No, I don't think so" I said, sitting up on the bed. The pain was beginning to subside.

"Summer, I need you to really think!" Reina is strategic but she loves games. She had to tell you something that could at least help us understand her plan. If I could figure it out, I can buy us time, possibly save our life."

I tried to think, but my eyes wondered down to my body. These weren't the clothes I had on. "How long have I been out?" I asked.

"5 days. You've been bathed and fed intravenously. Reina has had your nails and toes groomed and your hair washed and straightened.
I thought I had lost you when you didn't wake up, he said as he walked over to my bedside.

3 Unnerving

As TJ leaned over to kiss me on my forehead, I started to feel aroused. My heart was beating fast and I felt a throbbing sensation run through my body. I grabbed his hand and I placed it on my nipple. He looked down and me and we met each other's eyes. He knew that I wanted him. I was scared, it was the only thing I was certain that would calm my nerves.

I lifted my hands to unbuckle his belt, and then I unbuttoned his pants. I could feel his protrude as I pulled his pants down and began to gently massage his dick through his underwear. He groaned in pleasure and it turned me on.

I pulled his underwear down and I pulled him close enough to insert the tip of his dick into my mouth. He went wild, and wanted me more, but I grabbed his legs to keep him from pushing forward. I licked and sucked the tip of his dick softly, tongue kissing it several times before I let him lean forward.

When I did, he thrust his dick into my mouth forcefully and I gagged slightly as it hit the back of my throat. I pulled it out and licked his balls softly and his legs began to quiver.

He pulled his dick out of my mouth and pushed me back, grabbing my legs to pull me forward. He yanked off my panties and pushed my dress up over my bare titties. TJ got down on his knees and I felt the warm, wet, soft feel of his tongue sliding across my clit and I moaned out in intense pleasure. I immediately let cum slide from the center of my pussy walls and TJ did not bother to stop. He continued to pleasure me immensely and inserted his two fingers into my ass.

I pushed my body in a scooting position hard, which gave a combination of the wetness of his tongue and the pain of his fingers. I groaned at the pleasure that I felt. My clit clutched his tongue which caused a contraction of my ass to lock his fingers inside the walls. I grabbed his head and I forced his face further into my pussy. I rocked my body back and forth and found continuous pleasure in the warmth of his tongue and the pain of in my ass. And I relaxed all of my muscles as I felt the eruptions of my organs travel down my walls and collapse through my pussy. I belted out a language that had no origin and I filled his mouth with a gush of orgasm, so much that it filled his outer mouth area and leaked out rapidly.

He stood up and pulled just my bottom half up on the bed so that I was half up, half down, and he thrust his dick inside me and I orgasmed again as he positioned me so that each time he pulled his dick back he would rub my G spot. I moaned out in pleasure and begged him not to stop and it drove him wild.

He flipped me over and forced my head and back down, only propping my ass in the air and he stuck his dick into my pussy and his fingers in my ass.

I gasped in pain and he didn't stop. I orgasmed again and groaned from the pleasure that I felt from the transition of the pain. He increased his speed of thrusting and he cried out in pleasure.

He gave a final thrust which was so hard that I felt like his dick would come through my pussy and out of my stomach, and he filled me with cum that poured out of me over the bed. We both fell over, and I drifted off.

4 Distractions

I had a nightmare and it caused me to jump up out of my sleep. My head was throbbing again, and I could still feel the wetness of my orgasm from TJ.

TJ, he wasn't there. He was missing. I leaned over the jail like bed to reach for the light, thinking maybe he would be sitting in the corner across the room thinking about how to get us out. But, as I flicked the little lamp on and it dimly lit the room, there was no sign or TJ.

I turned to scoot out the bed and my leg felt the warmth of a liquid. I wasn't surprised because I was sure it was from my leaking pussy. When I looked down, I realized that it wasn't. It was blood and I panicked.

I hopped out of the bed and ran to the door, banging, screaming. "Help me, somebody help me please!!!"

There was nothing but an unnerving silence. I started to sob. "I am going to die here" I thought. Just as I was backing away from the door, a note slid under the door.

No one can hear you scream. You'll cause undue stress to the baby.

"I'm not having this baby you fucking psycho! Let me out of here!" I screamed. I felt the throb from the injury to my head and I leaned over in pain. I became dizzy and I must have passed out because everything went black.

"I'm dreaming", I thought. I felt the intense pleasure from the wetness of saliva on my clit and I thrust my bottom downward toward it. I immediately felt the hands grab my legs and pull them down holding them steady so that the lips of my pussy were pulled back and only my clit was exposed. I moaned and opened my eyes.

"TJ?", I said. Silence. The room was dark, and I couldn't see. Suddenly, I felt a presence standing over me. I could see a figure, but I couldn't make out who it was. The figure leaned over me and I could feel the hardness of a penis tough, my side. He began to suck my tittes so softly. I moaned. The pleasure was uncontrollable and the adrenaline from fear didn't help. I wanted so badly to not enjoy it, but I didn't want the feeling to stop. It was like a drug.

A third person? I saw another shadowy figure enter the room. Moments later I felt my arm pulled up and a sharp pinch just as I exhaled an intense release of cum into the mouth of this mystery man.

I was being picked up, carried. They were moving me somewhere, but everything was so hazy. "I think they drugged me", I thought to myself. As I was going in and out of consciousness, I caught glimpses of what seemed to be a hall. It was some sort of material on the walls that resembled sponge like cotton, the kind you see in a recording studio. Then, I saw *her*. She was walking along side of whomever was carrying me, poised and beautiful as always. This psycho bitch was always in control and that was my first mistake, thinking that I was a step ahead of her. She looked down at me and we locked eyes right before everything went black.

The brightness of the sun shining through woke me up. I thought I was dreaming. Perhaps it was a way to escape my reality. But, after a few minutes I realized that I wasn't dreaming at all.

I was in a king size bed. The room was beautiful, and it resembled the room I had at Reina's house. The pillow top blanket was pulled over me neatly as if I had been tucked in and the pillows beneath my head smelled of lavender, but the room smelled sterilized, like a hospital.

I sat up immediately and looked around the room. For a moment I felt like I was going crazy. I couldn't tell the difference between what was real and what I was dreaming. I was scared.

As I scoped my surroundings, I noticed a giant trunk with a bow on it and a note at the foot of the bed. "What the hell is in such a huge trunk?" I wondered. I swung myself around to the side of the bed in an effort to get out of it.

I had been bathed. The black silk gown I was wearing was clean and my hair had been pulled back in a ponytail. I felt weird, but I attributed it to all of the drugs Reina must have had pumped into my system.

My head was bandaged, and my nails and toes were manicured. There was an IV pole hanging beside the bed. "What they hell" I thought to myself.

I pulled myself to the side and stepped out of the bed, heading toward the end where the trunk was with the bow. When I arrived at the trunk, I pulled the card off and read it.

I trust that you enjoyed the meal supplied to you last night. The product you left on the sheets says that you certainly did. Summer, distractions are dangerous. I've decided to give you another chance now that they are gone. A gift for you to remember how much I care about you. - Reina

I pulled the trunk open and there were two carefully wrapped boxes. One was large and one was small. I picked the large one up first and sat it on the bed. "This is my way out, all I have to do is pretend long enough for her to trust me again, and I may make it out of this alive", I thought.

For the first time I felt a small glimmer of confidence and I sighed in relief. I tore open the gift box and as soon as it was opened, I jumped back and screamed. My legs felt weak and I was shaking uncontrollably. I was scared before, but this shit made before pale in comparison.

TJ's head sat in the box, on ice, and when I opened the box his eyes were the first thing I saw. I sobbed immensely and fell to the floor. I crawled over to the trunk and pulled out the small box.

"No, no, no", I whispered before opening the box. When I got the box opened, there it was in 4 plastic baggies. I could see the little fingers and toes, and then I saw the head in a separate baggie. It resembled a small toad, but I knew exactly what it was.

I slowly took my hand and lifted it to my panties where I felt the cushion. Looking down hesitantly, I moved my gown and pulled open my panties. The pad with the blood in it was enough to kill me of heartbreak.

Reina had aborted the pregnancy and I did nothing to stop her. For the first time, I realized that I did love the baby and I wanted it. Tucked to the side was a recorder with a tape.

The note on the recorder read *Play me*.

I pressed play on the recorder. " Dum, dum, dum". It was a heartbeat and I knew without having to be told that it belonged to my baby.

I sat paralyzed with emotion on the floor beside the box. I couldn't cry, scream, move. I just sat there. This bitch was not only psycho, but she was evil, and I was scared. TJ could no longer save me, and I didn't know what I would do. For the first time in my life, I prayed. I didn't know if there was a god, and if there was, I surely was not worthy of any of his attention, but it was all I had left.

I didn't want revenge; I didn't want to die. I just wanted to get away. I closed the box, placed it back in the trunk and stood up to close the box with TJ's head in it. I placed the head back in the trunk and closed the trunk.

I crawled back into the bed and I laid there. For the first time I didn't cry. I didn't scream. I just laid there. My mind was blank, and it was the first time in a long time that I didn't feel fear. I didn't feel anything. I was empty.

5 Emptiness

I watched the sun come up and go down so many times that I lost track of time. I didn't move, not even when people came into the room to check me and clean me up. I didn't respond to the questions about how I was feeling, half the time I didn't even blink. At some point the trunk was removed from the room, but I didn't even turn my head to see who was dragging it away.

I was still, limp, as they lifted me to wash me and dress me like I was a rag doll. My hair was washed and combed, my nails neatly manicured, and then my toes. I must have been in some sort of psych ward, because it was evident that everyone around me had gone fucking crazy.

The same people never came in twice and I didn't recognize anyone. Reina hadn't been come in the room at all. But, how could she? How would she be able to look at me, knowing that she had killed every piece of me? She might as well had just killed me physically, because I was already dead.

I don't know how many days had passed when I heard the door to the room open in the middle of the night. I didn't even open my eyes to bother seeing who had entered. I had become accustomed to people coming in and out. However, it was the first time in a long time that someone was coming into the room at night.

I felt the cover being pulled back from my arms and I felt the warmth of breathing over me. Hopefully they were coming to kill me, finally, and give me peace. It was evident I was never getting out and Reina had proved so well connected, that I could literally be in this room until I died, and I had no one that would come look for me. She had killed anyone who would be looking for me.

"Summer?" I heard a whispering voice say. "Baby, open your eyes."
But I didn't. I kept them closed and stayed very still, hoping the culprit would either kill me quickly, or leave me alone.

"Summer?" I heard again. "Wake up baby, I'm getting you out of here. We have to go, but we have to go now" the voice whispered with a strange sense of urgency.

"Wait a minute, I recognize the voice", I thought. "It couldn't be".

I quickly opened my eyes and my heart dropped. My eyes swelled with tears not because I was happy, or sad, but because I knew that I had gone crazy. There was no way that this was possible. I had been stuck here and had given up on ever being found.

"How?" was the only word I could squeak out.

"There is no time, I'll explain later. We have to go now; we may not have this opportunity again" Maddie said. There was someone with her, but I was unable to make out the figure.

The figure was scurrying around the room looking for something. "Where are her clothes?" he asked.

"We'll take her like this" Maddie responded as she was lifting me out of the bed. "Can you walk" she asked, looking at me.

"I, I, I don't know. I haven't been out of the bed" I responded.
Maddie pulled me to the side of the bed, and I tried to stand, but my legs didn't work. I couldn't feel any feeling in my legs. Fear was the first waking feeling I'd had in days.

The figure came over to the bed and he helped Maddie lift me out of bed. He bent over and scooped me up as if I was an infant who he was about to put to bed. It was the first time I was able to see his face clearly.

He was gorgeous. His skin complexion was the same as mine and he had a wave like texture hair. He had some Asian like traits, but he looked Black. He was gorgeous and his body felt very muscular. He felt very familiar, but I was sure I had never met him. But at that point, any glimmer of hope would have confused me.

"He looked down at me and I swear I saw his eyes tear up. "What has she done to you?" he asked rhetorically. But I didn't answer, I just laid my head on his chest where I relieved an overbearing amount of emotions that was building up.

"We can't take her out like that, it's freezing outside. Summer, are there any clothes that you could wear? Maddie asked.

I thought very hard about the sounds I would hear when people would come into the room and my eyes found the corner of the room where a chest sat. "I think there are clothes in that chest by the wall, but I'm not sure" I said in a whisper. My throat felt dry and raspy.

Maddie rushed over to the   chest and opened it. She pulled out a thick housecoat and some socks. The gentleman sat me on the bed while Maddie placed the socks on my feet and then pulled my arms through the warm housecoat. I didn't realize how cold the room was until I felt how warm the housecoat was.

She wrapped the housecoat closed around my waist and the gentlemen picked me up again and we headed toward the door of the room. My heart was beating so fast that I almost had a heart attack. The fear was paralyzing, and I didn't want to think about what would happen to Maddie if Reina caught her.

As we slipped into the hallway there was an eerie silence. The light seemed so bring, although I knew it was just regular lighting, and I felt like we were moving in slow motion, even though we were running.

I could tell Maddie and the gentleman were scared. As we ran through the halls, hiding behind the corners when we heard someone, I prayed. I asked the god that I was unsure existed, if he could intervene. It would take a divine intervention for us to get out alive.

The hallway was so long. It felt like we were never going to get out and I almost gave up hope. At every turn we were minutes from getting caught and I held my breath, expecting one of the Generals to catch us. I didn't know where we were, but I recognized several voices I heard. Black, Tan, and Luiz in particular. I could hear Luiz moving along the corridor providing direction that had been issued out from Reina. If anyone would catch us, it would be him. He was Reina's seer, and he would surely tell her that they had come for me.

Just as I was giving up, Maddie pressed a door with an exit sign, and I felt the cold crisp night air. A quiver ran through my body from the cold, but I was so happy to be outside that I didn't even care.

It looked like a fortress. There was gating surrounding the building, but the place was beautiful. The lawn was well kept and there were fountains shaped like angels with harps that spilled water in a rotation. The entire building was glass and it overlooked the ocean. I had never seen this place before, as long as I had known Reina. I had no idea how Maddie would even know to find me. She knew even less about Reina than I did.

We were out, but we were still running. "The car is just up past the bushes there" Maddie said pointing toward a dark hedge.

"We're almost there" the gentleman said as he looked down at me. We were moving fast, and my heart was beating fast.

Suddenly, I heard the alarm sound and I looked at Maddie in fear. I could see the look of panic on her face and as I looked up, I could see people running with guns through the glass windows. I began to cry.

Just then, I heard Reina's voice call out from behind. "Maddie, what the fuck do you think you're doing? You betray my trust?" she said. Then I heard a sound like a M80 firecracker, and the gentleman dropped me and fell over me.

"Oh my God!" Maddie said in panic. The gentleman rolled over, grabbed a gun from his pocket, looked at me and said, "Summer, you have to run, can you get up?

I shook my head and I was on my feet. He looked at Maddie and said, "GO!"

"I'm not leaving you here!" Maddie responded. He moved his hand from his stomach, looked at Maddie and said, "I'm already dead. I'll hold her off".

Maddie yanked my hand and we ran. It sounded like the 4th of July behind us and it seemed like we ran forever.

We got to the car and Maddie hopped into the driver's seat. I got into the back seat behind Maddie and she pulled off like a rocket ship. I laid still in the back seat of the car listening, as the car sounded like a game at the carnival, until   there was silence.

I could hear Maddie crying in the front seat, but I was too scared to lift my head in a pathetic excuse to comfort her. I just stayed on the floor like a coward and prayed.

After what seemed like an hour into the drive, I felt wet ness on my side. I slid my hand down to my side and scooped the liquid, then I felt a terrible pain. I groaned out in pain.

"What's wrong Summer?" Maddie asked. "I don't know "I responded. "I have a pain in my side", I said, and then everything was black.

7 Twisted Reality

I woke up to a fog and looked around. I started to cry; it was all a dream. I was still in this hell hole I thought as I looked around the room at the elegant artwork. As the tears streamed down my face, I turned my head to the side to see the IV administering drugs through my arm and I felt hopeless. I pulled my arm toward me and began to rip the IV out.

"Summer, no, no, you're ok", Maddie said. I looked up at her and I burst into tears and started screaming.

"Stop stop stop! I screamed. I was afraid. I was losing my mind and my reality was warped.

"It's ok baby, I'm so sorry", Maddie said, as she sat beside be and took my head into her bosom.

"Wait, this is real", I thought to myself. "Mama?", I whispered.

"It's me", she said, and we just hugged each other and cried for several moments without saying a word.

I was safe. Mama had saved me, even when I had given up on thinking I'd ever get out. I had never felt so happy in my life, yet I was still afraid. I was afraid that it wasn't real, it was some sort of twisted reality that I had locked myself in from all of the drugs Reina had been pumping into me. Maybe it was the only escape I could conjure up. But, at that moment, I didn't care. I was with Mama and even if it wasn't real, it gave me a chance to feel safe.

"Summer, I don't know where to start", Mama said as she looked at me through tears. "I am so sorry that it took so long to find you", she said.

As I was looking at Mama, there were so many things that I realized was different about her.

Mama seemed older, exhausted almost. She was still extremely beautiful, but she wasn't quite the Mama I remembered. How long had I been gone?

"Mama?", I asked. "How long have I been gone?", I asked, looking into the lines that had appeared in her face.

"Summer, you have been missing for eleven months", Mama responded. "I thought Reina killed you, but then I caught a break. It wasn't until then that I found out you were still alive and where you were. Reina's reach is long, so I needed someone I could trust to help me", she said.

Then I saw that familiar sadness appear in Mama's eyes. "Summer, when we came for you a month ago", she started.

"A month ago?", I asked, startled.

"Summer, you've been in a coma for a month", Mama said sadly. "The man that was carrying you when we got out, was shot. The bullet went through his back, came out of his chest and through your side. We are very fortunate that you survived it. I thought I lost you again", she said.

I was confused about so many things. I had been missing for almost a year, and then I had been in a coma for a month. It only seemed like days to me that any of these things had happened. I had lost time, so much of it.

"The man who helped me save you, his name was Haru", Mama said before swallowing as if she were saving herself from being choked, "And, he was your birth father".

I didn't know what to think. A man whom I'd never met before had lost his life to save mine. Not only had Reina taken away what I loved most, she had taken away anything else that I could ever grow to love except Maddie.

"Summer, we have to kill her. She will not stop until we do", Maddie said as she looked at me. Her look had gone from sadness to vengeance. I had never seen this side of Mama and it was scary, yet familiar. Looking at my Mama in that very moment, I saw Reina, and I was afraid of her.

I moved out of Mama's arms onto the bed and I was paralyzed in fear. I don't know if I was more scared of the fact that I might lost Mama and be all alone, or the fact that the evilness that lived inside Reina lived inside of Mama. If Reina had taught me anything, it was that anyone with that type of evil was capable of anything. I knew then that I had to get away from Mama. I didn't trust her, and I was afraid of her.

Mama looked at me with confusion, as if she could read my mind, but she didn't say anything to me. She stood up and walked over to a table where she pulled off a tray of food and started walking it over to me.

"Here, I had some breakfast prepared for you" she said as she looked down at me with an awkward smile. She placed the tray on a connector beside the bed and pulled it over me, then she helped me get sat up so that I could eat.

"My throat is so sore", I said to her. "It feels like I've eaten a snake, just raw", I continued.

"I'm pretty sure it's from the incubator tube that was removed this morning. It will take some time, but you should heal up pretty well", she said.

"Maddie, thank you for everything", I told her. It was the first time since I had seen her that I had called her Maddie and not Mama. I could tell from her face that it was not something she was comfortable with. But, she responded, "You're very welcome baby", and exited the room

8 Healing Process

The days drifted away from me, but never the thought of Reina. I was up now, moving around and there was no confinement to the room. I could come and go as I pleased, but I never left the house. I wasn't sure if I was able to, but I also had no desire to.

Maddie spent a lot of time meeting with people who I'd never seen before, planning, waiting for the right time to kill Reina. It was almost as if she were fixated on bringing the existence of Reina to an end. It was the most peculiar thing ever. I knew that Reina was one of the most evil people that walked the earth, but she was still Maddie's daughter. I think that was what bothered me the most.

Things grew more awkward between Maddie and I as I distanced myself, planning my escape. I thought about all of the options I had. I knew that leaving Maddie would mean increasing the possibility that I would be found and killed by Reina, but there was no way that I could stay there.

The reality was, I had no one. My last living parent was murdered to save me, and my sister was as evil as my niece. Reina had taken the one thing in my life that I could call my own away from me and I still felt that emptiness.

My life was a wreck. And, although I was happy to be alive, my healing physically did nothing to improve my mental state.

Every night I had nightmares and woke up in sweat, praying that I would not see Reina standing over me with a 9MM. Oftentimes, I'd hear the heartbeat of a baby in the distance and I'd wake up, afraid of what I might see. I saw TJ headless in my dreams more times than I cared to be privy to.

The restless nights were never-ending, but on the outside, everything was coming together. I had resumed my poise posture and I found myself always well composed, just like Reina.

Every day I woke up and groomed myself extensively, even though I knew I wasn't going out. Maddie had a trainer brought in for me and I worked out fiercely. I listened more and talked less.

Eventually, I learned to move about the house at night without being heard.

Maddie had certainly had a major come up. She didn't partake in coke anymore and she was very calculated. Her home looked like a castle and it was well armed security around every corner. Although I wasn't a prisoner, it felt like I was living in a well decorated prison. There was alarms everywhere and I was not allowed to do anything without always having a pistol in close proximity.

Maddie was very impressed with my shooting and defensive fighting skills during our training sessions. She didn't realize that I had been training with Reina for quite some time and I had the capability of a killer. Somehow, she still thought I was the sweet baby that she had once raised. She assumed that she was teaching me skills that I hadn't already learned. I don't think the thought every crossed her mind that I ran a major drug and prostitution business. Those skills were a requirement to survive One thing I learned from Reina was, being a woman in the business meant you had to be better, smarter, and faster than men, or you'd never survive.

I knew the day would come when I'd have to face Reina again. At first, I dreaded it, maybe it as the fear that capsulated me. But, eventually, I grew to look forward to it. There was no way that I could continue being a prisoner.

Besides, as the days grew, I knew that I wanted nothing to do with Maddie anymore. I also knew that I would not be able to face her, the woman who had taken care of me, and ultimately saved my life, to tell her that I wanted her out of my life.

I was convinced that it wasn't until I completely rid myself of my psycho ass family, that I would be completely free. Still, there was a nagging sadness about leaving Maddie, Mama, alone. After all, she really had no one either. She had been alone her entire life, and all she had was me. Thinking about it only left me confused. I need to clear my mind. It had been a minute, and there was only one way I knew how to do it.

9 Training Day

He was incredible. He wasn't what I was used to, but nonetheless, gorgeous. His name was Alex. 5'9, about 220 pounds of pure muscle, gray eyes, low fade, and a baby face. He reminded me of a little boy pretending to be a man.

Alex had to be about 24, which was much younger than my taste usually, however, I was starving, and he looked like a steak to a hungry lioness. He was very quiet and did as Maddie instructed me. If he were remotely attracted to me, he didn't let on at all.

I remember the first time I saw him. Maddie brought him into my room and told me that he'd be my trainer. I remember thinking, this man is a god and it sent every tingle that existed through my body. I smiled at him, but he didn't smile back. He just got right to business, often working me harder than I cared to be worked.

I wasn't oblivious to the fact that he was being paid to train me and this was a job for him. From the looks of the sneakers her wore, I knew that the money he was being paid was probably a come up for him. He wore Champions, a brand I had never even heard of. The clothing that he wore to train in had no names that I'd recognize, therefore, probably not of any value.

As I got to know him, I saw that he was smart, significantly smarter than I thought. He was in school to be an Occupational Therapist and had hopes of training the athletes. His conversations were only enough to answer my questions, which made it very complicated to pull information from him.

But I was patient, and calculated, a trait that I had picked up from Reina. I knew I couldn't rush with his type; he'd be reluctant to share with me because technically, I was "still his boss's daughter" and he needed this job.

Pretty soon it became impossible for him to resist me. He'd show up for our training sessions and as soon as Maddie was out of ear shot, he'd pick me up and prop me against the wall.

Laying against the wall with my feet on his shoulders, my panties would be pulled down slowly, and he would fall to his knees beneath me; he'd eat my

34

pussy so passionately and softly, as if he were tongue kissing it for the first time.

I'd push down on his mouth, wanting him to press his face into me harder, but he'd resist the request. It drove me crazy and it prolonged the eclipse of the orgasm that awaited beneath his tongue. His tongue as always so warm, and wet. Every lick made my pussy throb and my nipples hard.

Sometimes I'd even lick my own nipples, being driven past crazy in the excitement for what I felt between my legs.

He was very predictable, so I knew what to expect. After I would let off the warm salty cum into his mouth from my throbbing pussy, he'd carry me over to the bed. Once I was on the bed, he would lay me down and insert his rock-hard dick inside of me. We didn't use protection. I don't know why, we just never did, not even the first time.

It was something that felt safe about him. He would pull out and empty his nut onto my stomach; sometimes right before he was ready to cum, I'd pull him out of me and suck his dick until the taste of salt filled my mouth, all of it.

He was a love maker. His kissed me passionately and sucked my titties softly, perfectly. He kissed my neck and my forehead as he pumped his dick in and out of me. He was so large that he filled me inside and every thrust hit my gspot over and over again. Being with Alex meant cumming over and over again, repeatedly. And I moaned out as quietly as I could, biting his lip and piercing his back with my nails.

I was his first anal experience. He didn't know fucking until I taught him to fuck me in the ass. The first time I asked him to flip me over he inserted into my pussy. I moved forward and opened my ass for him.

He was confused and had no idea what to do. I turned to him and said,

"Put your dick in my ass, take your finger and play with my pussy until I cum". But the minute he inserted into my ass he let off a sound that would have alerted the entire house if it weren't so damn big and nutted immensely.

He was drained afterwards and fell onto the bed. I crawled up him and over the top of him, let my bottom down and placed my pussy on his mouth. He sucked my clit and I rode his face slowly and passionately while I caressed my titties, spoiling my nipples, orgasming into his mouth and on his face. When I attempted to get us, he locked my pussy onto his face and continued to suck my clit, while he slid his finger into my ass. I pushed on his finger hard, which jolted my clit against his teeth, and I filled his mouth with my glory again.

These ended up being our days. Afterwards we would clean ourselves up and then we would engage in a strenuous workout as if nothing ever happened. By the time Maddie arrived to show him out, we'd be full of sweat from the workout, and appearing almost as perfect strangers.

I lost track of time. The days turned into weeks, and then into months. Alex and I became a norm for each other.

In the beginning he had a girlfriend, but that changed quickly. I doubt if she was able to compete with the sexual experiences that I offered him. I opened his mind to orgasms from places that he didn't know existed. It was because of me that he perfected eating pussy and ass appropriately.

I can only imagine what she must have thought the first time he inserted his finger into her ass. No doubt he hooked her, and now he was hooked to me. I knew in the long run it would lead to heartache for this young boy. But it was about an appetite that could only be satisfied one way and that ruled everything in my world.

I sucked Alex's dick so many different ways, licking his balls and playing with his nipples. He discovered that he could cum from having his ear licked after being with me.

I taught him different angles of me, from riding his dick with my ass in his chest to bouncing on his dick sideways with a constricted pussy muscle, causing him to let out moans and speak language I had never heard.

Alex left his boyhood and became a man with me. He wasn't aware of my capabilities, because we were so close in age. But I was so much older mentally and sexually. He soon found out.

"Summer, run away with me", Alex asked me as he looked at me seriously. I was stunned by the question and left speechless.

"Come on, you can't stay locked in here forever. I don't know what happened in your past, but you deserve to be free from it all", he continued. "Free from it all", I thought to myself. He didn't know what he was asking.

"I know I'm not as rich as your family, but I work hard, and I could take care of you. I'd work and you could find something that you love. I know there has to be more to you than meets the eye", he said.

I couldn't bear to tell him that I couldn't run away with him and I wasn't even sure that I wouldn't. He offered me another way out, free from Maddie, from Reina, and it was appealing.

"Where would we go?", I asked. His eyes lit up with hope. "My family owns a cottage on the beach in Mexico. We could live there until we found something of our own", Alex said as if every word was thought through.

"Let me think about it", I told him and kissed him goodbye. Shortly thereafter Maddie appeared with one of her security guys to escort him out. He was gone, but my thoughts weren't.
I knew there could never be a future with him, but he could be my way out and it was worth a great deal of thought.

10 Another Year Older

"Happy Birthday to you, happy birthday to you, happy birthday dear Summer", Maddie sang.

I opened my eyes. Time was passing me by and I had lost track of it. The weather was gorgeous outside, and it was my birthday. I didn't even notice, and I had nothing to celebrate.

I hadn't been out of the house in two years. Maddie came and went as needed, but she never traveled alone, and she mainly moved around at night. The closest I came to the outside was standing or sitting on the balcony outside of my room.

Alex was still coming but we hadn't talked much about running away together since the first conversation. I guess he felt that I would tell him when I was ready.

We continued the routine of making love and I became very fond of him, but I was too damaged to love him. Deep down inside I knew that loving him would be dangerous.

"Thank you", I said smiling at Maddie as she walked the cupcake with a candle in it to my bed. I blew out the candle, after making the wish that I was free.

"I was thinking that we could go out somewhere today", Maddie said as she looked at me hopingly. I looked at her in disbelief.

"Somewhere like where?", I asked her suspiciously.

"Well, Summer, you've been cooped up on his house for two years and we've had no sign of Reina anywhere. My ears to the street say she has stopped looking for you. Besides, we're so far away from where she is. I think it would be good for you to get out. All of this being cooped up can make a person want to run away", she said laughing.

I smiled at her and agreed. She kissed my forehead and told me to get dressed and meet her downstairs.

As soon as she closed the door I hopped out of bed and scrambled around the room, searching. Maddie used "run away". It was no coincidence that she used the same term I had used in a conversation with Alex and I had been with Reina long enough to know that coincidences were rare. In my heart I hoped that I was wrong, but in my mind, I knew I probably wasn't.

Ten minutes into my search, I found it, disguised as a jewelry box. It was a top-notch type of two-way radio. Maddie had been listening to everything.

That meant that she also knew that I was fucking Alex all along and she continued to allow him to come. I had given Maddie an advantage without knowing it.

At some point I trusted Maddie about as much as I trusted Reina. I wasn't sure when she had become the enemy to me, but she had. I hated her and Reina and I wanted nothing more than to free myself from her.

I guess she felt the same way. She had bugged my room, and maybe I was now her prisoner. I was pissed at that point. She had freed me from a monster, but she was a monster too. I made up my mind. I was leaving with Alex and she would never see me again.

Getting out was actually refreshing. Maddie and her security team took me to an upscale Mexican restaurant. It was quiet and empty. The décor was extremely expensive and the menu extensive.

We had dinner, drinks, and they all sang happy birthday to me. I had actually had a good time. Just before they started singing Happy Birthday, Alex was brought in. It would have been a nice surprise if I hadn't known why she actually did it.

He wasn't aware of what I had found out, so he completely acted cordial as if our relationship was strictly professional. Finding a seat between Maddie and I, he sounded a "Happy Birthday" in an employer/employee relationship type of way.

Alex looked gorgeous. He was dressed in an Armani suit, with Christian Louboutin loafers on. He had a fresh cut and his cologne could be smelled from the door. I had never seen him like that before and I wanted him badly.

It took everything in me not to stare at him. Sitting so close to him made my pussy wet and it was uncomfortable knowing that Maddie was so close. I felt like she could smell my pheromones.

"Excuse me, I need to go to the ladies' room", I said to the table. Security stood up to escort me.

"Alex, would you accompany Summer to the ladies' room and wait for her?" Maddie asked.

"Sure", Alex said.

It was if he and I were on the same page. As soon as we reached the bathroom, he followed me inside and locked the door. When I turned around, he kissed me on my lips with a slight bite, and pulled up my leather min I skirt harshly.

I had never seen this side of him, but I was aroused immensely, and I let him take control.

He pulled down my lace red panties and lifted me onto the sink, my body forward. He leaned to raise my shirt, pulling my tittie out of my red lace bra, and bit my nipple painfully.

I flinched from the pain, but he didn't stop. He got on his knees and slid his tongue across my clit, and I pushed down from the sink onto his mouth, which dropped me off the sink to a standing position.

He ate my pussy with his head up between my legs with my heels on and I engaged in a slight ride to his face. I grabbed his head and I exploded into his mouth, but he didn't stop. He continued to eat, and I quivered, falling back on the sink in an effort to not fall. I left off an explosion into his mouth again accompanied by a severe moan of pleasure.

He stood up, turned me around roughly and folded me over the sink. He picked the bottom half of my body up and inserted his dick into me.

His grasp was so rough that I hollered out in pain as he thrust into me so hard. He bit my back in excitement and he fucked me forcefully. Alex grabbed my hips so hard as he pumped his dick in and out of my pussy, that I knew there would be a bruise later.

His dick became rock solid and I knew that he was ready to release his pleasure so I tried to pull up so he could let off on my ass. But his grip was too tight, and he was excited. Before I could move, he filled me up and he groaned at the amount of pleasure he felt.

I leaned up from the sink and pushed him off me. I stood there looking at myself in the mirror with him in the background with his eyes closed enjoying the explosion he had just experienced.

We said nothing to each other. We cleaned ourselves up and returned to the table as if nothing had happened.

Once the night had ended and Maddie and I returned home, I went to my bedroom to bathe and get in bed. I could not stop thinking how Alex had nutted inside of me and what could come as consequences of that. That emptiness that I felt so regularly had become more prevalent.

For the first time in a long time I slept all night. When I finally work up, it was after noon and the sun was high through the picture windows that surrounded my room.

It had been a long time since I had slept so well and I didn't dream, about anything. I climbed out of the bed and walked to the balcony door. As I opened the door, the sun felt good on my skin and it put me in a good mood.

I sat on the balcony in my gown and enjoyed the view of the river and the trees. I inhaled nature and let my imagination take me away. I just sat there through late afternoon before I decided to get up and shower.

I showered, put on my workout clothes, and placed my hair into a nice sleek ponytail. Then, I grabbed the tray that had been left on my bedside and enjoyed my afternoon lunch at my table until Alex arrived.

Today was different. When Maddie disappeared outside of the door, we didn't attack each other. Instead, I took his hand and led him to the bathroom.

"Oh, so you like the bathroom action?" he asked, grinning ridiculously.

"I brought you in here because there is a bug in my room. They can hear everything discussed and I wanted to keep this conversation private", I said looking at him seriously.

His disposition changed quickly, and a look of concern crossed his face. "They have a fucking bug in your room? What is this prison?!" he asked angrily.

"It's a long story and I don't have time to explain, someday maybe, but not today. Were you serious about running away and living in your family's cottage?" I asked.

"Very!" he said seriously and grabbed my hand with sincerity.

"Then I'll come", I said matter of factly.

"Really?", he asked excitedly.

"Yes, I will", I told him.

We spent our scheduled workout time developing an escape plan. Everything had to be perfect and it would be nearly impossible for him to get on the property of he wasn't scheduled.

42

It had to be during a scheduled workout session, or I would have to tell Maddie about the relationship she already knew about. We would need to make it seem like we were going on a date. That would give us the opportunity. We put the plan in motion.

When we came out of the bathroom, we talked about telling my mother that we were in a relationship and asking her to allow Alex over more often than just workout sessions. The entire conversation was fabricated because we depended on the fact that she would be listening in.

I went down to the library where Maddie was reading contently on the couch and sat across from her. She looked up and smiled at me pleasantly.

"Good morning Sunshine", she said.

"Good morning Mama, I have to talk to you about something", I told her watching for her reaction. I could tell she was pleasantly surprised at the fact that I had called her Mama instead of Maddie.

"Ok", she said sitting up straight smiling in reassurance.

"I don't know how you might feel with the fact that this has been going on under your nose, but it's become kind of serious, so I wanted to talk to you about it. Alex, the trainer, and I have developed a fondness of each other", I blurted out.

"Well Summer, that's wonderful! I'm shocked it didn't happen sooner. You guys are so close in age and he's a good-looking guy!", she said as she got off the couch and rushed to hug me.

"I'm glad you're finally coming out of your shell and starting to live again!", she continued.

I hugged Maddie back., tightly. I knew that I would be leaving her forever and never returning. She had been the only family I had ever known. And, no matter what, I loved her. She had mothered me, and she had saved me.

Maddie was Mama. She was the best mother she could be to me under the circumstances and I could not help but fill with sadness, so I started to cry.

She hugged me tighter, but I knew that she was hugging me because she thought I was happy. Maddie had no idea that I was not the same and I saw her different. Being with Reina did that to me. I could no longer trust my mother because she had too many traits of her psycho bitch daughter.

I had to move on. I would be alone. Alex would help me get out, but I could never be with him. He was too fragile, and I knew that he would be a liability to me as long as Reina was alive.

Reina was calculated, smart. She was quiet, but I knew she was planning. She would eventually find me and kill me. It was only a matter of time.

I guess a part of me wanted to save Maddie too. If I was away from her, she wouldn't die trying to protect me. Maybe Rei would show her mercy.

Then there was the part of me that missed Rei. She was my best friend and I wished that I had not found out so many things. If I had just handled things a different way, we wouldn't be here.

Instead, I was trying to take control over a world that I did not fully understand. She had been operating in that world forever. I had no right.

I released Maddie from my embrace and looked at her with a question.

"We'd like to go out on a date, a real one. You think that would be ok?" I asked innocently.

"Absolutely, Paco can drive you guys anywhere you like, except the city. I cannot risk it; Reina has people everywhere" Maddie replied.

"Got it, no city!" I said excitedly.

Maddie looked at me, and for a moment, I thought I saw a glimpse of sadness. "Summer, if you like, you and Alex can go stay in the cabins for a couple days. It would be a nice getaway. It gives you a change of scenery and it's ducked off", she continued.

"Really?! "I asked in a stunned tone. "That would be awesome!" I continued.

Maddie looked at me seriously, "Summer, I'm going to kill Reina. I think it's a good idea that you're somewhere safe in case things don't go as planned."

"No Mama", I said, "Don't, just leave it alone. We're happy, and we're free" I said worriedly.

"Summer, we cannot truly be free until my daughter is dead. She will never stop looking for you. I had the opportunity to spend some time with her. It's how I got close enough to plan for your escape. She is evil. I have no choice" Maddie finished in a very matter of fact tone.

I began to cry. I had fucked up again. I feared Mama and all she was trying to do was protect me. Somehow, along the way, I had become a selfish bitch.

I sat back down beside Mama and I begin to cry. But this time I was crying for a different reason. I was scared to lose Mama.

Leaving her alive was a very different feeling than thinking of her dead.

"I can't let you do this Mama. I won't. This is my fight and I will not leave you to it" I said as I looked at her sternly.

"Summer, asking you to go to the cabin was a courtesy. Pack your things. I will send a car for Alex. You leave tonight" Maddie said as she stood up and headed toward the door of the room.

I tried to follow behind her, but she quickly exited the room and I heard a sound I hadn't heard before.

It was the sound of the door being locked.

I reached for the knob and tried to open the door, but it was locked. I started to bang on the door and call for her through the tears of sorrow of all the bullshit I had caused.

After 15 minutes of the tantrum. I realized it was pointless and I went to call Alex.

His phone rang and rang, but he didn't answer.

I was in a hurry to re strategize the plan. I was going to save Maddie by killing Reina first, or I was going to die trying.

11 Motion Sickness

It seemed like the time stood still, sitting there, locked in the room waiting, pacing, trying to figure out a way to save Maddie.

I couldn't bear to let another person die because of me, most of all because no matter what was going on, she saved me, even when I had lost all hope living.

Finally, I heard the lock on the door turn and Alex entered the room. He was smiling ear to ear and had his suitcase packed. As soon as he saw me he rushed to me with a worried look on his face.

"What's wrong?" "Are you having second thoughts?" he asked me, concerned.

I motioned him into the bathroom. He knew that whatever I needed to talk to him about was private, and we could not risk being listened to.

"Maddie is going to go after Reina. I can't let her do that alone. Reina is dangerous", I said to him in a worried tone.

"Summer, she is a grown woman, and from the looks of things, she can take care of herself. Look how much security it is around here. Don't do this. Let's stick to the plan; I don't want to lose you."

I pitied Alex for his gullible ways. He genuinely thought I was going to be with him and I could feel his love for me in every touch. I didn't want to hurt him, but it would always be collateral damage in the world and I couldn't dwell on his feelings.

"Alex, Maddie is all that I have left in this world. And I know you don't understand from all of the things I've told you about her and her daughter, but she doesn't deserve this. This is all because of me", I told him.

"Summer, dammit, it's not because of you! When will you stop blaming yourself? This is because of HER! She abandoned her daughter and you will only be a casualty of war! Let me save you" Alex said as he grabbed my hand.

I got a feeling in my gut and my internal alarms went off. Every time someone had tried to save me from something, it ended up being someone I couldn't trust.

Maybe it wasn't even the that. Deep down inside I didn't think I deserved to be saved. Ro was gone because of me and so was my baby. I made decisions based on my own salvation and didn't think of anyone else. I was no better than Reina. She wasn't the only one that deserved to die.

"Okay, let's go" I said to Alex and got up from the bench where I was seated.

He pulled me close to hug me, while resting his head on my stomach. He didn't deserve what I was planning to do to him and the guilt almost consumed me in that moment.

He turned into my stomach and slid my leggings down slowly, while looking up at me. I rubbed his hair to reassure him that he was being received.

Once he pulled my leggings completely down and I stepped out of them, he lifted one of my legs on top of the bench and the other to support me. Alex nibbled at my belly button area and then slid his tongue down to the neatly waxed area of my pussy that protected my clit.

I moaned and he grabbed my booty cheeks to pull me close and planted his tongue onto the lips that covered my clit. He was sensual, every lick, and his tongue was warm and wet. I was read to cum all over myself and he hadn't even touched my clit yet.

I pushed in, and squatted to position my body into a seat on his mouth and I felt his tongue insert into my pussy. I glided my pussy back and forth over his mouth in a slow riding position, causing his tongue to slide across my clit long enough to be near climax, but not long enough to release.

I felt Alex grab my booty cheeks and insert one finger into my pussy, and one into my ass and I clinched my cheeks from the sudden mild pain. The clinch caused my pussy muscles to contract just as his warm tongue glided over my clit, and I let out an aggressive moan, grabbing his head and holding it to that position. And I felt myself relieve an orgasm that started in the midst of my soul. Alex was going to push back, but I didn't let his head go. His restraint against my hold caused a clinch again and I filled his face with cum for a second time.

I released him to move and he crawled from under me. I fell to my knees gently while holding on to the bench. He crawled up behind me and grabbed my thighs. I pressed up against the bench in an effort to keep my balance, and I felt him insert inside of me.

He kissed my neck and my ear, while massaging my titty, and he fucked me sensually from the back

This position caused every stoke to rub my gspot and I moaned out the song of love making. Alex fucked me even softer with every moan and we did not care that if someone walked past the door they would hear.

He moaned out, "Summer, oh baby, you're going to make me cum".

I pushed him out of me and he fell on his back. I backwards crawled over him and sat down quickly and powerfully on his dick. He cried out in excitement and it drove me wild.

I rode him like slowly and I made every arch in my back work. He was shaking and so was I because my gspot was repeatedly being hit and my entire body was tingling.

He grabbed my hips to try to stop me, but I continued to make my pussy muscles contract and we reached our peak together, moaning out in pleasure. He filled me and the mixture of him and me spilled out of me.

I fell over on the side of him on the floor. I had never experienced the feeling I had right then with Alex before and I doubt he before me. Alex made love to me.

After getting cleaned up we sat on the bed and waited. Neither of us knew what time Maddie would have us moved, but we were prepared to put our plan into motion.

Finally, the lock turned and Maddie walked in. As she walked toward me, I could see the sad look in her eyes.

"Summer, it's time", she said as she pulled me close to hug me. I began to cry and I hugged her tight.

"Thank you Mama. Thank you for everything you have ever done for me", I told her sincerely, through my tears.

"Summer, look at me", she said sternly. "This is not forever and don't worry about me. I will kill Reina, and then I will come for you to tell you that you are free. Do you hear me?" she said.

I shook my head in agreement, but I knew that the reassurance Maddie was giving me was not even something she had. We both knew how smart Reina was and how incredibly powerful she was.

"Mama, how did you get me out?" I asked, without knowing that the question was going to come out.

"I traced your phone to her house and I planned. I knew that I had to get close to her. That would be the only way that I could get to you. I knew that she would have you wherever she was."

"I also knew that it wouldn't be easy to get her to trust me so I called your birth father, Haru, and enlisted his help".

"There was no way Reina would trust me, ever, but I knew her weakness".

Reina had a weakness? Who would have thought? I had to know what that was.

"Mama, what was her weakness?" I asked.

"Love", Maddie said and she motioned us to follow her.

Alex and I loaded into to the black SUV with two heavily armed guards. I watched out the window as our bags were loaded into the truck and Maddie delivered orders to some of the other guards.

It began to rain as we pulled off. I watched the trees as we drove, which seemed to wave goodbye to us.

Alex grabbed my hand and I looked over at him and smiled. Maybe I could just leave with him and be happy. Being with him in that moment made me feel differently about him.

Is it possible that I was in love with Alex?

My stomach began tying itself in knots, the feeling that resembles motion sickness. The thought of loving Alex was scary for me. The last man I loved had been taken from me, and I had vowed to never love again.

Alex pulled me over close to him in the seat and I laid my head on his chest. I kept is placed there and I felt safe, so I stayed.

It was a long ride, I was tired, and then I was sleep.

"Babe, we're here" Alex said, shaking me gently in an effort to wake me up.

I woke up feeling more rested than I had been in a long time.

The guards came around and opened our doors, allowing us to step out. They escorted us to the cabin, which was immaculately gorgeous.

I knew Maddie had inherited majorly after the passing of our mother, but I didn't imagine what magnitude. Her castle house that I lived in hiding, and now this cabin, it's was insane.

The cabin was on 4 acres of land and had a beautiful lake in the back. The statues on the side of the stairs probably were abut fifty thousand dollars apiece; and they were carefully hand sculpted.

There were six Master bedrooms, three regular bedrooms, and four bathrooms. The kitchen was custom for a chef, and the sitting room had an amazing fireplace.

It had a library with hundreds of books and an indoor pool area. There was a private in home theatre with theatre seating, and an indoor basketball court.

Maddie had the cabinets and fridge stocked with food, enough for survival during a natural disaster. If I didn't want to be free, I'd definitely want to live here. This cabin was better than Reina's house, and that looked like a palace.

It kind of made me sad. All the time invested in Reina's business, and I had nothing to show for it. I had no money of my own, no family, no business, nothing.

Even Maddie, who was a coked our prostitute most of my life, was doing better than me. It was a true self-reflection moment.

The guards brought our bags in and we got settled.

It was cold there so I knew that Alex and I would need to be warm because hiking through the 4 acres of land just to get to the main road, would cause us to freeze to death if we were under prepared.

After dinner I prepared some tea for everyone. I made a separate batch for the two guards, but I served everyone at the same time, careful not to mix the cups. Afterwards, we all chatted and laughed at each other's corny jokes before Alex and I said we were ready to retire to our rooms.

The guards escorted us to our room, went in first to check it for any sort of safety compromise, and then cleared us to come in afterwards.

We said goodnight, and as soon as the door was closed, we began collecting the necessities to travel.

"Summer, it's freezing outside, so make sure you put on enough clothes" Alex said.

"Where the hell are we anyway? It was warm where we left" I asked.

"Canada", Alex said as he grabbed his socks.

"We will hike out the land to get to the main road. Once we are on the main road, we can get a cab to take us to the bus station. We can't travel by plane because it's too risky, Reina has eyes everywhere." I told Alex.

"Here, I got the fake passports.", Alex said handing two passports to me.

We should be able to use this to get bus tickets to take us across the border and then, once we are back in the US, we will use them to get on a cruise. That is how we will get into Mexico." Alex replied.

We waited until the house was quiet and we put the plan into motion. I could hear the guards in the front of the house laughing and joking, so Alex and I headed toward the back door.

As soon as we stepped onto the back porch, he brisk air from the lake hit me in the face. I pulled my hood over my head and we began the hike.

"Summer, don't forget to get rid of your phone" Alex said through strained breath from us attempting to walk through the heavy winds.

I pulled the phone out of my pocket, threw it on the ground and stepped on it. I didn't even think about that. It would be just my luck that Maddie had already began tracking us.

It was two hours before we reached the main road and hailed a cab. I was grateful to get into the warm cab and relaxed as we headed toward the bus station.

Everything went smoothly and we loaded onto the bus to New York when we heard the call across the speaker. We made sure to avoid all cameras and not be memorable.

I didn't fully relax until we pulled off. As soon as the bus departed, Alex grabbed my hand and gave it a squeeze. I smiled at him. We had made it.

We made it to New York, booked the 10 day cruise to Mexico and started our journey.

12 Freedom

The next seven days were the best days of my life. Alex and I made love often. We barely came out of our room for air, and ate mostly room service.

We had a room with a balcony and spent a great deal of time out there enjoying the beauty of the ocean.

The weather was perfect and we spent a lot of time making love with the balcony door open, enjoying the breeze from the cruise ship. Alex loved me, and I let go and loved him back.

Finally, I had found happiness. I had hoped Maddie was ok, but I knew that I would never be able to call to check. In order to be free, I had to leave her behind.

Alex showered me with attention and I learned to enjoy it, without worry. I was almost sad when the time came for the ship to dock.

"We're here, we made it" he said as he kissed me on my forehead. "Ready to start our life together?" he asked me grinning.

"I've never been more ready", I said as I leaned in to kiss his soft lips.

He took my hand and escorted me off the cruise ship. Once we were off, we got on a tour bus to the city.

Looking out the bus window, it definitely wasn't what I thought it would be. The streets were raggedy and the people were poor. But, the ocean was everywhere, and that was enough for me.

Alex translated to the tour guide's words to me, pointing out all of the beautiful places in the city. None were as extravagant as I was used to. Mexico would definitely take some getting used to.

Once the bus stopped at a souvenir place Alex and I took our things and he flagged a cab. He spoke to the man briefly in Spanish, and then opened the door for me to get in.

The drive was about 45 minutes and it was grueling because the cab was dirty, small, and the dirt roads were extremely bumpy. The cab driver had some annoying Spanish music playing on the radio and he lit a cigarette.

The smell made me feel like I had to vomit and Alex could tell. Alex yelled something to the cab driver in Spanish and he discarded the cigarette out of the window.

Alex looked at me and mouthed "I'm sorry" and then rubbed the side of my face. I smiled at him and grabbed his hand.

We finally made it to our destination. I thought we could rest, but Alex told me that we had to take a fairy to get to his family's cottage. I mustered up the strength and got on the fairy.

Fortunately, the fairy was much better. The water offered a cool breeze, they played American music, and served us free drinks.

I enjoyed the ride across the ocean and being able to relax. I leaned back against the seat and watched the ocean as Alex told me of his family's heritage. He was talking, but I heard nothing really. I was happy to be free, to be genuinely loved.

Once we arrived at the cottage Alex escorted me up the stairs to the door. His cottage looked like it didn't belong. It was a gorgeous cottage, very dreamy, and modern.

It was surrounded by palm trees and it had sand and the ocean just out the front door.

The cottage had expensive paintings, four bedrooms and four bathrooms. It had a very motherly kitchen area with modern appliances. The cottage smelled clean, as if it were recently cleaned, and had fresh towels.

"My family has a cleaning service that comes in weekly to clean and ensure the cottage is always ready should we decide to stay", he said.

He took my hand and led me on a tour of the cottage, explaining the artifacts and paintings, along with the history behind how the things were acquired.

Afterwards, he walked me out to the front, down the stairs, and into the sand.

"Smell that?", he asked, as he smiled at me.

"What?" I said, smiling.

"It's the ocean, it brings peace", he said, as he picked me up to carry me down to the water.

We unpacked the little things we had and then split up to get showered and cleaned up. Afterwards, I cooked him Cajun jambalaya and fried chicken; then we made love on the floor in front of the sofa.

Alex made us cocktails and told me corny jokes. We made love some more and I filled his mouth over and over with the sweet liquid of my pussy.

He bent me over the couch, sat me on the couch and pulled me forward while he inserted into me, lifted me up against the wall and held me there, sat on the couch while I rode him until he erupted inside of me, and finally we landed back on the floor on the blanket.

He helped me get showered and cleaned up because I was so tired I could barely walk, and then he carried me to the bedroom.

I was exhausted, but Alex seemed full of energy. He laid me in the bed and then climbed in beside me. He stretched out his arm and I found my space in his chest. Minutes later I was sleep.

13 Finding Myself

I had never slept so deep in my life. I dreamt about everything, from the beginning with it was just Mama and I, to my time period with Reina, and then TJ.

I dreamt about a baby that looked so much like me, but acted just like TJ. I saw the ocean and the sun, and everything in between. And at the foot of it all was happiness.

I saw glimpses of Alex's smile and it made me smile, and flashbacks on Roosevelt. Alex and Ro were so different, but they both gave me what I so desperately needed, genuine love.

I realized that love was more prevalent than any of the riches I'd been accustomed to. I mean, Maddie had loved me, the only way she knew how. But even she loved me for a reason, my mother asked her to.

Then there was Reina, she loved me, in her own way. I truly believe she did. If I had been loyal to her things would have never turned out the way they did.

Maddie's words stuck with me. Reina's only weakness was love. I had failed her, and although I couldn't change it, I wished that I could.

My dream was revealing so much to me that I had missed in life and as I floated around the dream, I knew that this time around I would do things right.

I planned to be good to Alex, to love him, to bear his children. Maybe we would even get married. I had finally got a chance to start over.

I felt a breeze that was cool enough to make me shiver and I opened my eyes. I was still very groggy, but I saw that Alex was carrying me.

He saw that I was opening my eyes and he looked at me and smiled, "Hey sleepy head". I smiled back.

"Hi", I said, half asleep, unable to wake myself fully up. "Where are we going?"

"I have a surprise for you my love", he said and leaned in to kiss me.

I must of drifted off again because I was back in dream land.

I don't know how long I must have slept , but it felt like days has gone past when I finally woke up.

I opened my eyes, but my head hurt so badly. I was pretty sure that I had over did it on the cocktails. It could have even been us acting like jackrabbits all night.

When I opened my eyes I could see I was in the bed, but the room looked different. It certainly was not where I went to sleep at.

"Alex?" I called out. "Alex?" I called out again before attempting to get up.

I was tied down, to the bed. I completely woke up and then I saw Alex. He was standing next to the door of the room, leaning against the wall looking at me.

But, I didn't see anyone I knew. He was somebody different.

"Hi Summer", he said, and then he flicked on a television.

Maddie appeared on the screen, seated in a chair with a rope tied around her, gagged with a cloth. There were five dead men laying around her chair.

I immediately recognized the men standing over the bodies. It was the Generals, two of them specifically, Tan and Black.

I started to panic and I was squirming to get out the rope when I saw it, the sound of the television so loud, it sounded like I was standing next to it,

Maddie's brains out of the front of her head. The gun was held by a neatly set of manicured nails and I knew who they belonged to.

The sight paralyzed me and tears slid down my cheek.

Maddie 's body dropped out the chair on to the pile of the other body and the television screen went blank.

I looked at Alex in fear as he walked over to me.

He removed the gag from my mouth and I started to scream. He hit me in the head with a metal object and everything went black.

I woke up in the trunk, my hands and feet were bound, my mouth taped and all I could do was cry. I tried kicking the trunk, the seat, but there wasn't much room for me to move.

Finally the car came to a stop and the trunk opened. Alex stood there, looking at me smiling, and he picked me up and swung me over his shoulder. I tried to scream through the tape, even to move, but he had bound me too tight.

He walked about two miles into some type of forest area and then he stopped at a freshly dug grave. Tears were running down my face and I was praying.

Alex turned his head toward me, looked at me as if he didn't know me, and said, "My boss sends her regards." before dropping me into the grave.

As Alex began to fill the hole where he had discarded me like trash with dirt, my entire life flashed before my eyes. Reina had been ahead, again, all along. She knew how to beat me because I was her. She knew we would have the same weakness, love. I knew I was about to die, but I was finally free.
It felt like forever, but I knew it was only actual minutes before my air ran. out.

ABOUT THE AUTHOR

Going by the pen name Queen, she is a new author who enjoys writing urban erotica. Queen wanted to bring something different to her readers, not just erotica, but a capturing storyline. Her vision were inspired by so many urban writers that came before her to open doors to a taboo imagination. She began writing the first book as a hobby, never intending to publish it, but found a love for getting lost in the storyline and the Summer Series was born. Follow Queen Novels through the journey by liking the page on Facebook @NovelsbyQueen